A Her
Welcome

Ndidi Chiazor-Enenmor

Walnut
Publishing Limited

www.walnutpublishing.com.ng

A Hero's Welcome

Ndidi Chiazor-Enenmor

Published in 2019 by Walnut Publishing Limited

Ikota, Lekki, Lagos, Nigeria.

Reprinted 2020

info@walnutpublishing.com.ng

ddlconsultancyng@yahoo.com

Tel: +234 8023083218 +234 8095286514 +234 8039158632

Illustrated by Wale Adebiyi

Cover design and page layout: Femi Adedeji

ISBN: 978-978-972-351-5

Printed in Nigeria

To children, all over the world, who speak their native languages.

Chapter One
A Proper Breakfast

Mrs. Ofochi gently taps at Enyinna's bedroom door. She pushes it open to peep at her sleeping son.

"Enyi! Wake up. We have a lot to do today."

Enyinna opens his eyes, yawns, then sits up on the bed.

"*Ututu oma*," he greets his mother, his voice groggy, as he rubs his palms across his eyes.

"*Ututu oma nwa m*," she responds fondly. "Tidy up and come over to the kitchen," she says, strolling away. As soon as his mum leaves, Enyinna flops on the bed again and covers himself up with the duvet. He soon drifts back to sleep.

He did not sleep early the previous night. He had stayed up late, ironing his mum's clothes. He had also cleaned the kitchen, washed the bathrooms and the toilets. It was almost midnight before he finished the chores and went to bed, tired and exhausted.

There is no house-help in the Ofochi's household. Enyinna and his sister are used to house chores. Mrs. Ofochi does not believe that a **male** child should be exempted from house

1

chores. "Since no child came to the world holding a broom in their hand, every child, male or female, should be brought up the same way", she always says.

About an hour later, Enyinna finally wakes up. The first rays of the sun are already peeping through the curtains. He yawns again. He is not in a hurry to get up from bed. He shuts his eyes again, hoping to fall asleep once more but the sharp pangs of hunger will not let him. He slowly gets up from the bed. He says his prayers, makes his bed and saunters towards the kitchen. The sound of his mother's chirpy voice is clear and strong. She is singing an Igbo song. Enyinna hums the verses and joins her in the chorus just as he reaches the kitchen door.

"Enyi, *kedu?*" his mum asks cheerily. She does not look up from the bunch of vegetables she is shredding. Beside her, in a bowl, sits an even bigger bunch of wet *ugu* leaves.

"*O di mma,*" Enyinna responds. "I slept very well."

Mrs. Ofochi is resolute in speaking the Igbo language to her children. She is happy that her efforts are not in vain. Conversing in Igbo has become a norm in the family.

Both her daughter, Ezinne, who is now an undergraduate at the university, and her son Enyinna, are very fluent in Igbo. They can all carry on a full conversation in Igbo. Mrs. Ofochi is very proud of this fact and does not miss any opportunity to educate other parents on the need to engage their children in their native languages. She believes that every child should grow up, speaking a local language.

"How can a child not speak a Nigerian language, when both parents are Nigerians?" she always queries, in her constant rebuke of her friends who speak only English to their children.

"The mother tongue should be spoken in every home. Children will ultimately learn English because it is the language of instruction in Nigerian schools," she always says.

Unlike many other families in their neighbourhood, the Ofochi children are among the few who understand and speak their language.

Enyinna looks around the kitchen curiously, wondering what his mum is preparing with the big heap of vegetables. Breakfast with plenty of vegetables does not look interesting at all.

"Mum, are we not having a proper breakfast this morning?"

"What do you mean by a proper breakfast?' his mother asks, still engrossed in her task.

"A proper breakfast must include bread, sausage, jam, cereals, juice and hot chocolate. Maybe *akara* and *akamu*, with plenty of milk. I mean something delicious to eat, not breakfast with so many vegetables. A proper breakfast should be fun to eat," Enyinna concludes gloomily, folding his arms across his chest.

"Who says that vegetables don't make for a proper breakfast?"

Enyinna sighs wearily. "What a way to start the day," he mumbles to himself. He dislikes food with plenty of vegetable. To have it as breakfast makes it even more disheartening.

He goes to the fridge for a glass of cold water, to calm himself from the sadness welling up inside him. He casts a glance at the dining table and his face lights up instantly. Nicely laid up in a large tray is a bowl of cornflakes, a tin of milk, a plate of scrambled eggs, a mug of fresh juice and a loaf of *Agege* bread.

"Oh! Mum, you were just pulling my leg," he says, chuckling.

3

"Mum, are we not having a proper breakfast this morning?"

"Yes dear, I was. The vegetables are for the *edikang ikong* that we will have for lunch. I hope lunch with plenty of vegetable is proper?"

"Yes mum." Mother and son burst into laughter.

"So, can I just brush my teeth and eat now, Mum?"

"Yes, dear."

Enyinna rushes off to brush his teeth. He comes back to the dining table afterwards.

"Mum, can I eat now?"

"Yes, my dear. Go ahead but the fresh juice is for both of us."

"Mum, I can't finish it, even if I were a glutton. I am more interested in the *Agege* bread than in the juice."

Enyinna loves *Agege* bread, so does his sister. It is a locally produced kind of bread made by small-scale bakers in Lagos. They are usually hawked on the streets. Enyinna used to wonder how the name, A*gege* bread, came about. His father had explained to him that many years ago, in Lagos, most bakeries were located in the Agege area. Now, there are bakeries all over the city of Lagos, offering different varieties of bread.

Mrs. Ofochi could not do anything to stop her children's love for *Agege* bread. When she buys sliced bread from the big stores, they remain uneaten for many days. Enyinna, in particular, will not eat a slice out of it. His mother eventually succumbed to buying *Agege* bread.

Mrs. Ofochi's initial concern about the bread was that they had no labels on them to show the name and address of the bakery. Secondly, the sellers often exposed the bread to flies.

Enyinna loves Agege bread, so does his sister.

But when she met Iyabo, an *Agege* bread seller, Mrs. Ofochi was impressed with the extra care she took to cover up her bread. Not only that, she wore hand gloves while attending to her customers. She changed the gloves at regular intervals. Now, Iyabo supplies *Agege* bread to the Ofochi's family three times every week.

Done with the vegetables, Mrs. Ofochi joins her son at the table. He is devouring the bread and scrambled eggs hungrily.

"Your dad has not called this morning," she comments, pouring herself a glass of fresh juice.

"Maybe he is already on the rig," Enyinna responds thoughtfully.

"Maybe. We should expect his call at night then."

Mr. Ofochi is an engineer with an oil servicing company, operating in the Niger Delta. His work schedule entails four weeks at work on the oil rig, then two weeks with his family in Lagos.

"Mum, thanks for the nice breakfast."

"You mean the proper breakfast?"

They both laugh heartily.

"We need to tidy up arrangements for your trip," Mrs. Ofochi states, in between sips of juice.

"I have already packed everything I need."

"Don't forget your cardigan. Lagos harmattan is child's play beside Owuama harmattan."

"Yes! Mum," he responds, getting up to clear the dishes.

Enyinna's grandparents will be celebrating their 50th wedding anniversary. The entire extended family has been planning the event for several months. Enyinna loves his grandparents dearly. He loves to spend time with them. He pleaded that his parents should allow him travel to Owuama one week before the event.

The holiday has been boring for Enyinna. His only sister, Ezinne is at the university, so he has been a bit lonely at home. He misses Ezinne. The universities ought to be on break too, but the lecturers' strike affected the academic calendar. Now, Ezinne is in school while he is on holiday.

He tries to occupy himself with activities. When he is not doing house chores, he watches detective films, his favourite kind of movies. Sometimes, he plays some games on his mother's laptop. Except for the visit he paid his best friend and class mate, Ibrahim, last week, there has been nothing special about the holiday. Enyinna loves the kind of life children live in Owuama. They play outdoors with one another; not indoors with gadgets. He really looks forward to the trip. It will be a relief from the boredom.

Chapter Two
Journey to Owuama

Early the next day, Enyinna and Jonah, the driver, are set for the journey. Mrs. Ofochi dishes enough jollof rice and plantain for them, in separate food flasks. It is going to be a long journey and they will definitely get hungry. She does not want them to buy food from the vendors on the way.

"The easiest way to get down with typhoid fever is to eat unhygienic food," Mrs. Ofochi always says.

Jonah has been with the Ofochis for as long as Enyinna can remember. He knows their home town. He has driven the family home for Christmas several times. He had also taken Enyinna's grandparents back to Owuama a couple of times, after their visits to Lagos. He is well known to the extended family members.

Jonah is a careful driver. He does not speed unnecessarily. This is the major reason the family has retained him as their driver all these years.

When Enyinna was little, he was taught in Sunday school

that Jonah was swallowed by a fish. For a long time, he thought that their driver was the same Jonah who was swallowed by the fish. He used to have a lot of sympathy for him, imagining what he did in the fish's belly for three days.

Recently, Jonah began to resume work rather late. He blamed it on the bad roads in his area which made it difficult to get a commercial bus out of the area. He pleaded with Mr. Ofochi to give him a loan to secure an apartment in a closer location.

"You will be taking the money out of my salary, sir," he had begged. Mr. Ofochi gave him the money, but not as a loan, rather as a gift. Jonah was very grateful for the gesture.

"You must take me to your new apartment. I want to know the place," Mr. Ofochi said. That was over seven months ago. Mr. Ofochi is yet to see the apartment. Each time he comes to Lagos, he gets busy with so many other things. On his part, Jonah seems not to be in a hurry to show his boss the new apartment he got.

Before getting into the car, Enyinna hugs his mum tightly.

"Bye, Mum. See you and Dad in a week."

As they drive out of the estate, one of the guards at the gate waves at Enyinna. He rolls down his side of the window and waves back. The guard is a very friendly young man and often exchanges banter with Enyinna.

"Enyi, where are you off to this early morning?"

"I am going to the East," Enyinna replies with a broad smile.

Among the Igbos in Lagos, a trip to any of the states of Anambra, Imo, Enugu, Abia and Ebonyi is often referred to as a journey to the East.

Enyinna gets his pen and notebook ready. He wants to write down all the towns they will drive through from Lagos to Owuama. He loves to observe things and to take notes about towns and cities he encounters on any journey. He will include as much details as possible in the essay on "How I Spent my Holiday." It is a regular assignment in his school after every holiday. Enyinna hopes that his essay will be the best this time. There is always a prize for the best essay.

Traffic is not so heavy this morning. When schools are closed for the holiday, traffic in Lagos becomes light. This is because there are no school buses on the roads, conveying pupils to school. Neither are there parents or drivers rushing to take children to school. Soon, they are in the Epe express way.

Enyinna remembers how he used to count the number of cars on the roads whenever they travelled out of Lagos. He used to do so with his sister. Each would decide on the colours of cars to count. "I choose white, red and blue," he would tell Ezinne. "You count the black, yellow and purple cars."

"How many cars have you ever seen painted in purple or even yellow?" Ezinne would protest. She would accept the challenge, just to please her younger brother. They usually got tired of counting in no time.

Today, Enyinna is not interested in counting cars. Apart from taking note of towns and cities, he also wants to observe the landscape and terrain. His geography teacher always talks about landscape and terrain.

Soon, they arrive Ijebu Ode, Enyinna writes it down, with an explanatory note that Ijebu Ode is located in Ogun state.

Enyinna observes that Jonah is unusually cold and distant today. Normally, he would talk with Enyinna, boasting of his driving skills. Once, he told Enyinna of how he drove from

Aba to Kaduna, non-stop.

"When was that, Uncle Jonah?" Enyinna had asked.

"Many years ago, when I was working with a construction company."

"How many hours was it from Aba to Kaduna?"

"About twelve hours."

Enyinna had expressed a lot of surprise that day.

"Uncle Jonah, you mean you drove for twelve hours without taking a break."

"Yes, I did not take a break. I only stopped two times to urinate. Once, at Otukpa in Benue state, and again at Akwanga, Nassarawa State."

"You mean Otukpo in Benue state?"

"No. Otukpo is different from Otukpa but both are in Benue state."

"So, you were not hungry?"

"I was not hungry at all." Sensing that Enyinna did not believe him, he added, "When you have something important to do, you don't think of food. I was driving to Kaduna to deliver something very important."

Today, Jonah is not keen on any conversation with Enyinna. He answered three phone calls in less than two hours, each time, speaking in very low tones. It is not his habit to answer calls while driving, especially on the high-way.

"Did you see that, Uncle Jonah?" Enyinna asks excitedly as a squirrel dashes across the road. Jonah nearly crushed the small animal.

"I did not see anything. It is only the road that I am seeing."

Enyinna opens his note book again and writes about the squirrel. It is very clear that Jonah is not in the mood to chat with him. He looks away quickly anytime his eyes meet Enyinna's through the inner mirror. "This is rather strange," Enyinna thinks. He decides to ignore Jonah and continue his observation of the landscape.

Soon, Enyinna falls asleep. He wakes up later to find that Jonah has pulled over. He is having a conversation with a man on a dark pair of glasses. He looks out for a signpost and sees that they are in Ore.

"Why did you stop, Uncle Jonah?"

"I stopped to greet my friend."

Enyinna takes a closer look at the man's face but his glasses are too thick and dark. Enyinna cannot make any sense out of the conversation between Jonah and the strange man. They speak in a different Igbo dialect which Enyinna is not used to. There is no warmth in their brief chat. Nothing suggests that they are friends. The man speaks in a squeaky voice which Enyinna finds odd and funny. He also has a foul body odour. Enyinna refrains from covering his nose, out of politeness.

Done with his chat with Jonah, the man walks off and Jonah restarts the car. Enyinna looks at the man through the side mirror. He observes that he walks with a slight limp. Unable to restrain his curiosity, Enyinna asks Jonah if his friend lives in Ore. Jonah ignores his question. Rather, he turns on the radio and begins to hum to the beat of the music coming from the FM station. Enyinna feels hurt at Jonah's attitude. He gets out his notebook and writes: 'Ore town in Ondo state, where Uncle Jonah stopped to greet his strange friend.'

A while later, he brings out his food and starts to eat. The

He is having conversation with a man on a dark pair of glasses

jollof rice is still hot, as hot as when his mother dished it. Jonah does not seem to be hungry yet, otherwise he will park the car somewhere safe to eat his own food. Enyinna does not want to ask him any more questions.

They drive past few Ohosu, a border town between Ondo state and Edo state. There is an interesting thing about this town. It is like two towns in one; known as Ohosu on the Ondo side but called Ofosu on the Edo side.

At Okada town in Edo state, Jonah pulls over to buy some plantains and garri. Enyinna knows that his mother gave Jonah money to buy some food items that they will take to Owuama.

"If you want to ease yourself, you can come down and do so," Jonah tells Enyinna, still avoiding direct eye contact. Enyinna goes to a corner to pee while Jonah haggles with the plantain and garri sellers.

Walking back to the car, Enyinna remembers the first time he knew that there is actually a town known as Okada. It was on a journey to Owuama, several years ago, with his parents and his sister. Curious and surprised to see a sign which read, 'Welcome to Okada Town,' he had asked his father whether the motor-bikes popularly known as *Okada* were manufactured in that town. His father had laughed and had explained to him that an illustrious son of the town, Chief Gabriel Igbinedion, once owned an airline known as 'Okada Air' which he named after his home town. With the advent of motorcycle as a means of public transportation in Nigerian cities, people nicknamed it *okada*, comparing its speed with that of an Okada Airplane. The story has never ceased to fascinate Enyinna.

Jonah buys two bunches of plantain and a small sack of

garri. He arranges them in the boot of the car, then he eats his food quickly and they set off again. At Asaba, the Delta State capital, Jonah drives into a petrol station. "I need to buy fuel," he stated.

Enyinna says nothing in response. He watches keenly, the hawkers rushing to the vehicles that drive into the petrol station. Each hawker displays their wares with pleas to be patronised.

"My bread is very fresh," says one. He is a good-looking young man with a lot of rings on his fingers. His nails are very long and unkempt, Enyinna observes, as he showcases the loaves of bread.

"Buy plantain chips," screams a young girl of about twelve years.

Done with the fuel purchase, Jonah waves off the hordes of hawkers impatiently. He quickly pulls out of the petrol station.

As they approach the Niger Bridge at Onitsha, Enyinna brightens up. He is happy that the long journey is gradually coming to an end. He is always captivated by the beauty of the bridge and the serenity of the River Niger.

There is a lot of traffic at Onitsha. Enyinna watches with interest as *okada* riders edge their way in-between cars, hooting loudly as though they are being chased.

"*Jili nwayo*," a passenger shouts frantically as the *okada* conveying her nearly bumps into their own car. The woman's plea for the rider to slow down is ignored as the *okada* speeds past.

Forty-five minutes later, they arrive Owuama. Enyinna begins to count the number of houses they will pass before arriving his grandparents' house. As they approach the compound, Enyinna closes his eyes out of sheer excitement. Grandma shouts in jubilation as she opens the gate of the vast compound. Enyinna leaps out of the car and hugs her. Grandpa smiles broadly as he walks to the car.

"*Nnoo, nnoo*," Grandma and Grandpa said repeatedly to Enyinna and Jonah. "You are welcome."

"You are just growing big every day," Grandma remarked, looking at her grandson closely, as if to measure the level of growth he has attained since the last time she saw him. She leads the way into the house. Enyinna drags his suit case along. There are two buildings in the compound. There is the traditional *obi* where Grandpa loves to stay during the day for some fresh air. He also receives visitors there, especially members of his age-grade. The *obi* looks quite old but Grandpa refuses any attempt by his children to renovate it.

"You can renovate the main house but leave my *obi* as it is," he has maintained.

The main house is big and imposing, with several rooms. Enyinna's father has done a lot of renovation on it. It has also received a new coat of paint in view of the upcoming anniversary. At another end of the compound is a small building. Part of it used to be Grandma's old kitchen, before the main house was built. Made of red bricks and old corrugated iron roof, the small house stands as firm as the mango tree behind it. Now, used as a store where Grandpa and Grandma keep many old relics, the elderly couple have refused to have the building knocked down or rebuilt. It holds many memories for them.

"I made *abacha* for you. I also made *ukwa*. Which one will you like to eat?" Grandma asks Enyinna and Jonah. Enyinna chooses *abacha* while Jonah settles for *ukwa*.

"But Mama Nnukwu, I will still eat the *ukwa* tomorrow."

"No problem my dear. I will keep some for you and warm it up tomorrow," Grandma assures him.

"Let them bathe first before they eat. They have had a long journey," Grandpa insists.

After a quick shower, Enyinna happily settles down to eat the *abacha*. He loves the meal a lot. It is made from cassava flakes. Grandma prepares *abacha* really well and she particularly spices it up with fish and garden eggs. In Owuama, *abacha* is eaten, both as delicacy and as a main meal. During every ceremony in the town, including traditional marriages, new yam festivals and burials, *abacha* must be eaten. It is a ceremonial meal.

Grandpa always has good conversations with Jonah anytime they meet. Tonight, he tries to engage him in a chat but Jonah shows no enthusiasm.

"How many hours was the journey?"

"About eight hours," Jonah replies curtly, swallowing some *ukwa*.

"That was quite fast," Grandpa says. "The roads are better now, I guess, especially the Ore road. Before, one could spend hours trying to navigate through Ore."

Jonah is silent. At the mention of Ore, Enyinna remembers the man on a dark pair of glasses. He is about to say something but at that moment Jonah belches loudly. He eats a little more of the *ukwa* and excuses himself.

"I will be returning to Lagos tomorrow," he says, getting up to retire to sleep.

"O.K. Good night," Grandpa says tersely.

Early the next day, Jonah leaves for Lagos before Enyinna even wakes up.

Chapter Three
Moonlight Games, Moonlight Tales

Enyinna loves Owuama for many reasons. One of the things he enjoys most is the moonlight games he plays with his age mates and playmates in Owuama.

Grandpa's big compound is a gathering point for children from nearby homes. Usually, after supper, they will start to troop in. The children love Enyinna a lot and are always happy whenever he is around. He speaks Igbo fluently and plays freely with them. This is unlike some other children of the town who live in big cities with their parents. When they visit Owuama, they are reluctant to mingle with the children in the village.

One of Enyinna's favourite games is *akpa nkoro*. To play the game, everyone holds hands together to form a big circle. They swirl around, happily singing the *akpa nkoro* song. The last child to squat at the end of the song leaves the game. It goes on till a champion emerges.

This night, Chinedu introduces them to a new game, *Kuru nmiri, kuru azu*. Only a few of the older children know the game. It is interesting but complicated. Each child stands on one leg and raises the second leg to intertwine with that of the next child. When this is perfected, they break into the song, *kuru mmiri, kuru azu*. They sway their bodies to the song, making motions with their hands, like fishermen paddling, catching imaginary fish. The singsong game continues like that until the children are tired.

"I am tired. My legs are paining me," Obiageli shouts out.

"Don't be lazy! We have not caught enough fish," Chinedu retorts, laughing.

When Ifeka and Akuabata also complain about tiredness, amidst heavy panting, they decide it is time to call off the game.

"It is story time now," Enyinna screams, running towards the spread out mat. He is followed by the group of giggling children.

Grandpa is already seated, waiting for them, in front of the old house. He had known as soon as they started the game of *kuru mmiri, kuru azu* that they will get weary easily and come running to him for tales.

Grandpa is always happy to tell the children stories from his repertoire of folk-tales. Enyinna often wonders if Grandpa's stock of stories will ever get exhausted. He has a different story to tell each night. He hardly repeats a tale except the children themselves demand that a particular story be retold.

"*Ifo cha kpii*," Grandpa begins, clearing his throat.

"*Woo*," the happy children chorus, every one of them itching to get closer to Grandpa.

"Once upon a time!"

inna often wonders if Grandpa's stock of stories will ever get exhausted.

"Time, time," the young audience chorus again. Grandpa, adjusts his chair, rubs his two palms together and begins the story.

"The flying birds of the air decided to learn a new dance. They met every day for practice. Tortoise begged to be accepted as part of the dance. He offered to play the drum for the birds. They allowed him and he really did a good job of the drumming." Here Grandpa pauses to ask a question. "What is the Tortoise known for in the animal kingdom?"

"His greed and tricks," the children scream.

"Good. We shall soon find out what happened between him and the birds," says Grandpa, adjusting in his seat again.

"So, one day, the birds were invited to a feast up in the sky and at that feast, they were to display their new dance. Tortoise, not having wings to fly, was at a loss as to what to do, because he wanted to be part of the feast. Surely, he did not want to miss out on the feast. Do you want to know what the tortoise did next?" Grandpa asks.

"Yes" the children scream in excitement.

"He pleaded with the birds to donate one feather each to him, to enable him to fly with them to the sky for the great feast. The birds considered the matter for a while. Since Tortoise was their drummer, they decided to oblige him with a feather each. Tortoise thanked them for their kind gesture. On the day of the feast, they had all assembled, beautifully dressed. That was when Tortoise began to think of a plan."

"What was his plan?" Chinedu asks, wide-eyed.

"Tortoise suggested that it would be a good idea if each of them picks a ceremonial name for the day. The birds applauded Tortoise for his wisdom and they began to choose names, one

one. When it got to the turn of the Tortoise, he said he would bear the name, 'All of you.' The birds considered the name strange but since that was his choice, they let it be. They flew to the sky for the great feast; Tortoise flew along with them in his borrowed feathers.

They all had a good time dancing. After much dancing and change of pleasantries, it was time for food and drinks. Their host had prepared so much. There were different kinds food, yam pottage, fufu, *nsala* soup, *egusi* soup and *ogbono* soup. There was also palm wine and pepper soup. When the host had laid out all the food, he announced that the food was for 'all of you.'

"And then?" wonders a child aloud.

Grandpa continues. "Tortoise sprang up immediately and declared that since his name was 'all of you,' the food was meant for him alone. The birds felt miserable. They watched in pain and regret as Tortoise ate up all the food. When he was done eating, he belched loudly and then went ahead to drink up the palm wine. The birds were really sad. They felt betrayed by Tortoise's action. They were very angry with the trick which Tortoise played on them. They decided to take back their feathers one by one. Each bird took back its feather and flew away. At last, only Tortoise was left. He didn't know what to do. His stomach was so filled with the food and the palm wine that he could hardly move. Darkness was fast approaching and Tortoise was really troubled. He must do something desperate to get back home."

"So how did the Tortoise return to earth?" It is Obiageli asking now.

"He decided to jump from the sky, hoping that he would land on soft soil. Unfortunately for him, he fell on very rocky soil and his shell was broken to pieces. He sustained so much injury that he had to nurse himself for days. He regretted the trick he played on the birds. He begged Spider to help him stitch back his shell. Spider did his best to stitch the shells together, using his web. That is why Tortoise's body is the way it is till today."

"Serves him right," Enyinna exclaims.

"It will teach him not to be greedy next time," quips Ebuka, the youngest child in the audience. He had managed to keep awake till the end of the story, just to know what happened to Tortoise.

"So my children, stay away from greed," Grandpa advised them, reclining in his chair.

By now most of the children are already feeling sleepy. It has been a long but interesting evening. They all thanked Grandpa for the story, bid one another goodnight and depart for their homes.

Chapter Four
Grandma and Friends

Grandma is a magnet that attracts people. She has many friends who have been paying regular visits to her, especially as the wedding anniversary celebration draws closer. Nne Agidi comes visiting today.

"Nne, *nno*," Enyinna greets the elderly woman, curtsying.

"*O nwa m*," she responds admiringly.

"*Enyi bute oche*." Grandma tells Enyinna. He runs off to get a chair for Grandma's friend. Grandma leads her friend to the outer courtyard. As soon as Enyinna brought the chair, Grandma instructs him again, in Igbo, to get some garden eggs for her and her friend. Enyinna runs off again to Grandma's kitchen to get the garden eggs.

Grandma's kitchen is quite large. There is a big cupboard where she keeps her cooking utensils. There is one big earthenware pot at a corner of the kitchen. The pot is used to store drinking water, fetched from the stream. Water from the pot is always cool because of the red mud underneath it. Both

Grandpa and Grandma prefer the water from the stream.

"Water from the fridge is too cold for our teeth. It makes t[]
teeth shake," Grandpa often explains.

Enyinna gets some garden eggs from the basket placed on t[]
of the cupboard. He washes them and places them in a sm[]
tray. Then, he opens the cupboard to fetch a knife. Grandr[]
and her friend will need to slice the large garden eggs in[]
small bits to eat. There is a small knife with a safety shea[]
which Grandma always uses for such purposes. Grandma h[]
kept the knife for years, even though it has become a bit rus[]
He returns to the outer courtyard and places the garden eg[]
knife and tray on a small stool.

"Ose *oji kwanu*?" Grandma asks Enyinna. She alwa[]
loves to eat garden eggs with groundnut paste. It is a go[]
accompaniment.

"O gwugo," Enyinna responds, surprised that Grandr[]
could have forgotten so soon that the *ose oji is* finished. S[]
ate the last of it last night with Grandpa.

Nne Agidi is amazed that Unoaku, her friend, is conversi[]
fluently with her grandchild in Igbo. Her own grandchildr[]
do not understand Igbo. Whenever they visit, which is not[]
regular, she finds it difficult conversing with them.

"Is it not the same Lagos that you and my grandchildren l[]
in?" she exclaims. Enyinna smiles.

"Enyi speaks Igbo very well," Grandma interjects, feel[]
very proud. "He even knows Igbo proverbs and adage[]
Enyinna feels amused. Grandma has a way of spicing up [
stories. He gets another chair for himself and goes to sit und[]
the big kolanut tree in the vast compound. He loves the w[]
the cool breeze under the tree teases his skin. From there, []
also gets a good view of passers-by. Grandma and her frie[]

also take their chairs to join Enyinna under the tree.

"I have told my daughter many times to teach my grandchildren our language. I almost bit my tongue the last time I visited Lagos, trying to speak English to them," Nne Agidi says shaking her head sadly.

Just then, a hawker passes by, in company of her dog. Grandma and her friend turn their conversation to the hawker.

"Is it not Ojiaku, the moi-moi seller?" Nne Agidi asks, stretching her neck to be sure.

"She is the one. Do you want to eat moi-moi?"

"No! I can't tolerate anything made of beans for now. My tummy has been upset for days now. But even if I want to eat moi-moi, I will definitely not buy it from Ojiaku. I can't eat any food from that woman because I don't know if it is cooked by her or by her dog, with the way that dog follows her about."

Grandma laughs. Enyinna chuckles.

Shortly after, Nne Ugomma walks into the compound, aided by her long stick. Nne Ugomma is one of Grandma's closest friends. Enyinna has always known Nne Ugomma with the walking stick. She always complains of pain on her legs. He quickly gets up from his chair. He takes it to Nne Ugomma to sit.

"My leg pains are getting worse by the day," she says as soon as she sits down. She places her walking stick carefully beside her, unslings her raffia bag and brings out a little bottle of kerosene. She applies it to her legs, sighing deeply. The smell of kerosene fills the air.

Enyinna feels concerned. Many elderly people in Owuama use kerosene as ointment for many ailments. They apply

"It is the same with me. I have not spoken to my daughter for a whi

erosene as balm for mosquito bites, cuts, bruises, even tooth che. Nne Ugomma sighs again. She puts the kerosene bottle ack into her bag.

"My medicine is finished so I have been using only kerosene. need my daughter Ifeoma to send me a new stock of medicine ut I have not been able to speak to her for some time. This hone is a burden when you cannot speak to your children ith it."

"It is the same with me. I have not spoken to my daughter for while," Nne Agidi says. "Even when she calls me, I hardly ear what she says because the line is always faint. And I need ר to send another bag of rice as quickly as possible. I cannot ait till Christmas."

"What of Osita?" Grandma asks, directing her gaze at Nne gomma. "Why don't you tell him to send you drugs if ɔu cannot get through to Ifeoma? I am not happy with the ɔndition of your legs. I am not happy at all," she emphasises, nding down to examine the legs critically. Enyinna is nused at his Grandma acting like a doctor.

"Hmmm! Osita, my son, I have not spoken to him in a long ne. Each time I call his number, that useless girl will be eaking grammar to me."

"Which useless girl?" Grandma and Nne Agidi chorus, most together.

"I don't know. It could be the girl he wants to marry. I am ɔpy that Osita has finally decided to get married. But I have ɔt even met her and she is already speaking grammar to me. annot explain why she is in possession of my son's phone. ave not approved that my son should marry her. My son nnot marry such a lady." She stamps her foot on the ground r emphasis.

Enyinna is surprised that Nne Ugomma could stamp her foot so hard on the ground in spite of her complaints of pain on her legs.

Nne Agidi claps in amazement. "How these girls behave these days is a shame. Does she not know that you are Osita's mother? Does she want to snatch your son from you? A son that you carried in your womb for nine months."

"But what exactly does she say to you on the phone?" Grandma probes further.

"She speaks grammar to me, grammar that I cannot understand. I am just holding my peace till I see Osita face to face."

"You cannot wait till you see Osita. No! You have to teach that lady a lesson," Nne Agidi says, flaring up in anger. "I say you must teach her the lesson of her life."

Nne Ugomma lifts up her hands in despair. "What should I do? Eh! My friends, what should I do?"

Grandma thinks for a while and brightens up. She beckons to her grandson.

"Enyi, please come. We need you to speak to this lady. Tell her to hand over the phone immediately to Osita so that my friend can speak to her son. Enough of her nonsense."

Enyinna braces himself for the task. He really feels sorry for Nne Ugomma. He asks for Osita's mobile phone number. Nne Ugomma produces a crumpled piece of paper from her bag. Enyinna manages to read out the number. He punches the digits on the phone's keypad. He turns on the speaker button so that Grandma and her friends can listen to his conversation with the lady. The call did not go through. Rather there is a response from the service provider, saying, "the number you are trying to call is not reachable at the moment, please try again later."

"Can you hear her?" Nne Ugomma shouts. "You have heard the silly girl speaking her grammar as usual."

Enyinna explodes in laughter. Grandma and her friends look at him, puzzled.

"Enyi, why are you laughing?" Grandma asks.

"That voice is a recorded message from the service provider. It says that the number cannot be reached at the moment."

"Oh, so it is not a lady in possession of my son's phone," Nne Ugomma says, looking relieved.

The three friends burst into a fit of laughter, joking about their ignorance.

Enyinna feels a sense of pity for Nne Agidi and Nne Ugomma. It could be frustrating for them, not being able to speak to their children for days and weeks. Network for mobile phone communication is really poor in Owuama. He thinks of what to do to help Grandma's friends. Sending text messages may help, he reasons.

He offers to help them send messages to their children, to inform them of their mothers' needs. Enyinna wants Nne Ugomma to stop using kerosene on her legs. That can only stop when she receives a new stock of her medicine. He carefully types the messages. Before the end of their visit, text message alerts come into their phones. Enyinna helps them to check and they are responses from their children.

Nne Agidi's daughter promised to send her mother a bag of rice in the coming week, through any of the commercial buses that come from Lagos. Both Osita and Ifeoma, Nne Ugomma's children promised to visit their mother the following week, with enough supply of foodstuff and medication. The two women are overjoyed. They are full of gratitude to Enyinna for solving their problems. Soon, they get up to leave. Grandma gets up too, to see them off.

Grandma returns with three other elderly women. Nne Ugomma and Nne Agidi had stopped to narrate their story to everyone who cared to listen. They were full of praises for Enyinna for his help. Now, Enyinna has more work to do. He listens to the elderly women intently as they narrate their needs to him, in Igbo language. He types the messages, then sends them to their children.

"Tell my son that my waist pain has started again, the medicine he bought for me is finished," one of the new arrivals says, handing Enyinna her phone which is tied with a rubber band. Without the rubber band, the phone will fall apart.

"Tell my daughter that the doctor is in need of the balance of his money," another one says.

"Tell Uchenna, my son that the roof of the house is leaking," the oldest-looking amongst them says wearily.

Enyinna happily sends their messages. He is just glad to be of help.

Chapter Five
Grandma's Missing Goat

Grandma has a black he-goat and a white she-goat. She wakes up early every day to cut fodder for them from nearby bushes.

Grandma's children have told her several times to give away the goats but she refused. They feel it is stressful for a seventy-two-year-old woman to be rearing goats. Grandma does not consider it stressful. She enjoys it. Apart from her husband and her friends, the goats are the reasons she hardly stays away for too long whenever she visits her children in the cities.

The bleating of the goats is not loud this morning. This is strange and gets Grandma worried. She goes closer to the pen and discovers that the she-goat is not there.

"*Alu emee!*" she exclaims. This draws Grandpa and Enyinna's attention. They both rush towards the pen to find out what the terrible thing is. Grandma's two hands are on her head. She is lamenting loudly.

"Where is my goat? Chai, *alu emee!*"

Grandpa checks round the compound but the goat [is] nowhere to be found. "The goat must have been stolen," he says thoughtfully. "I must get to the town crier's hous[e] fast. Today is *Nnukwu Nkwo* market day. The thief must b[e] apprehended before he sells off the goat."

Nnukwu Nkwo is the biggest market day in Owuama. [It] attracts sellers and buyers from both within the town an[d] other neighbouring towns. The usual market day is a fou[r] day cycle but *Nnukwu Nkwo* is on every eight day.

Enyinna offers to accompany Grandpa to the town crier['s.] They rush off, leaving Grandma who is now sobbing loudl[y.] "Oh, my goat, my goat," she cries repeatedly, beating h[er] chest.

Grandpa leads the way through the foot path which [is] shorter. Enyinna feels the dampness of the shrubs and gra[ss] touching his feet. The weather is cold this morning. He ru[bs] his palms together before folding his arms across his chest f[or] some warmth.

Birds are chirping and their noise sounds like music [to] Enyinna's ears. It reminds him of his visit to the Lek[ki] Conservation Centre with his classmates, the previous term[.]

Soon, they arrive at the town crier's home. It is a small hous[e] in the middle of a small compound. Enyinna is impress[ed] with the cleanliness of the compound. The town crier [is] cleaning his teeth with a chewing stick. He has the tradition[al] red cap on. He is bare-footed but seems to be getting set to [go] somewhere. He greets Grandpa.

"Nwokekaibeya! What brings you to my abode this ear[ly] in the day?" Nwokekaibeya is Grandpa's title. In Owuam[a,] elders are greeted and addressed by their titles.

Grandpa goes straight to the point.

"Udoka! Fetch me my ogene, fast," the town crier bellowed.

"My wife's goat is missing. It must have been stolen th morning because we still heard it bleating with the other or before we slept off last night."

"What colour is the goat?"

"White."

"He-goat or she-goat?"

"It is a she-goat, a pregnant she-goat. That makes two goa stolen, not one." Grandpa shakes his head sadly.

"Mmmh! And today is *Nnukwu Nkwo*."

"That is exactly my thought. I hope the goat has not bee sold off," Grandpa remarks sullenly.

"Udoka! Fetch me my *ogene*, fast," the town crier bellowe He throws away the chewing stick and wipes his mouth. H son immediately emerges from inside the house with th metal gong. Enyinna looks at the boy with pity. He is clad a torn singlet and a pair of worn-out shorts. He is bare-foote

"I will go round the town right away to pass across th information," the town crier says. He quickly washes his fa with water from a small bowl. Washing of faces, like chewir sticks, is a daily morning routine in Owuama.

Done with washing his face, the town crier springs in action.

"Nwokekaibeya! I am off. I hope the people who are yet leave for the market will get the information and hopeful the thief will be apprehended."

The town crier trudges off, beating his ogene and screamin *"Ndi be anyi gee nu nti ooo."* This catchy phrase from the tow crier asking the people to listen always stops people in the tracks. He then goes on to pass the information. Enyinna ar

Grandpa walks home while the town crier's voice punctuates at intervals along the way, relaying the information about Grandma's missing she-goat.

As Enyinna walks back home with his grandfather, thoughts of the town crier's son and his tattered clothes occupy his mind. The boy should be his age mate, he reasons. Enyinna is filled with compassion and as soon as they get back to the house, he rushes to his suitcase to pull out some clothes for the boy. He also takes a pair of shoes, a belt and a face cap. He packs them in a big carrier bag.

"I am going back to the town crier's house. I want to give these things to his son, Udoka," he announces to his grandparents. Grandma looks at him in disbelief. She has stopped sobbing over her missing goat.

"You will do no such thing, Enyinna. Wait till your parents come on Thursday."

"But Mama Nnukwu, all the boy had on him was just a pair of torn shorts and singlet, and he was even bare-footed."

"I said you will not step out of this house with that bag, Mr. Do-good. So you want to give out all these to a boy you hardly know?"

"Mama Nnukwu, I have lots of clothes in Lagos. I am just giving him two pairs of trousers, three shirts, one pair of shoes, one belt, one face cap and two…"

Grandma cuts him off.

"Why don't you give him your entire suitcase of clothes? You have become Red Cross eh! You think your parents are picking money from the streets. You think…"

"My dear wife, let the boy be. Don't stop a child from doing a good deed." Enyinna is glad for Grandpa's intervention.

"I am not stopping him from doing a good deed. I am only saying that his parents must approve of it first."

"I am very sure they will not mind. Don't you know our son and our daughter-in-law? That is how they give out things."

"Thank you, Papa Nnukwu," Enyinna says, taking the bag with him as he hurriedly sets off to offer his gifts to Udoka.

On his return, he finds a group of people gathered around his grandparents. They are talking at the top of their voices. He becomes worried, but on getting closer he sees that Grandma is beaming with smiles. Her stolen goat has been found and the thief apprehended. The town crier's information had quickly spread through Owuama and people were on the lookout.

The goat had been sold in the market but the innocent buyer was having a hard time transporting the animal out of *Nnukwu Nkwo* market. The vehicle he was to board had some difficult passengers already seated and they refused to share their space with a goat.

"We cannot share this tiny bus with a goat," complained the fat woman whose body had occupied the front seat meant for two. She did not seem to have a neck as her head seemed to just sit on her shoulder. Her arms were folded into layers, rolls of fat. Her voice was as thick as her looks.

"And a smelling he-goat for that matter," stated another passenger, covering her nose.

"It's not he-goat," the man had insisted. "It is she-goat. Can't you see that it's even pregnant?"

"If it's not he-goat, then why does it smell so foully?"

"Whether it is he-goat or she-goat is not my concern. All I know is that I cannot share this bus with a goat," retorted the fat passenger.

The driver's pleas to placate the women fell on deaf ears.

"You must refund our money if you must carry the goat," the fat woman had maintained.

The more the driver tried to pacify the women, the angrier they got. It was in the middle of the argument that someone came to the scene to whisper to the driver that the goat was a stolen one.

By then, a cluster of people had gathered to listen as the innocent man gave a thorough description of the person who sold the goat to him. From the description provided, it was clear to all that the culprit was Orinkemadu.

Truly, several people had seen Orinkemadu in the market very early in the day. He was dragging along, a pregnant goat, desperately looking for a buyer. He had left the market as soon as he sold the goat.

The innocent buyer narrated to the crowd, his transactions with Orinkemadu.

"I wondered at the price of the goat. I was thinking 'This must be my lucky day.' He didn't even refuse my counter offer when I haggled with him to pay lower. And he seemed to be in a hurry. I should have smelt a rat."

"Oh, so you paid the price of a rat to get a goat," the fat woman had interrupted him. "No, you should have smelt the goat." Everyone laughed except the man. He felt embarrassed and cheated. He had parted with his money and will not go home with the goat either. The goat was taken from him and as he walked away sadly, even the fat woman felt sorry for him.

The Owuama vigilante group immediately swung to action

He was dragging along a pregnant goat, desperately looking for a buye

to find Orinkemadu. He was traced to a drinking parlour in the neighbouring village. He was arrested instantly and taken to the Igwe's palace.

Enyinna reflects on Orinkemadu and his action. "He is living up to the meaning of his name," Enyinna muses. "Orinkemadu: one who eats what belongs to others."

Chapter Six

Arrivals

It is the eve of the golden jubilee. There is a flurry of activities in the entire compound. Family members arrive in trickles and then in droves. Enyinna is highly elated at seeing his cousins, uncles and aunts.

His parents came earlier on in the day. Enyinna is surprised that his father drove. "Jonah is not feeling well," his mother explains. Enyinna has never heard about Jonah being sick.

"That's strange," he thinks. He is about to tell his mother about the stranger Jonah spoke with at Ore, and his unusual quietness during their trip, but at that moment, some of his cousins arrive. He runs off to hug them. He helps them with their luggage.

Kelechi and his sister, Chisom, live in Kano with their parents. Enyinna is particularly close to Chisom. Enyinna's mum also comes out to welcome the newly arrived family members. She hugs Chisom and her brother and asks them about their journey in Igbo. Chisom and Kelechi stare blankly at her. Mrs. Ofochi turns to their parents.

"Don't tell me you don't speak Igbo to these children." She looks pointedly at her brother-in-law.

"How many hours in a day do I spend with them?" he replies laughing.

"The little time you spend with them; you should engage them in Igbo language."

"But it's not easy, especially as their mother is Ijaw," Uncle Uzo replies. He knows how passionate his brother's wife is about speaking local languages.

"Well then, I hope she speaks Ijaw to them. Do you?" Mrs. Ofochi asks, this time, turning her gaze to her sister-in-law.

"It is not easy at all," Kelechi's mother responds as she throws her arms up in the air. "I am Ijaw, their dad is Igbo, and Edna, my house-help, is Berom. It makes it so difficult, so we simply communicate in English and life goes on."

"They would have been speaking these three languages easily if you, Uzo and Edna had engaged them consciously in them. Young children have the capacity to speak up to five languages, and even more, if they are exposed equally to those languages as they grow."

"Really?" Uncle Uzo exclaims.

"Yes, research proves this fact. Children learn easily when they are young. It becomes more difficult to learn a language when they are fully grown."

She continues to speak as the other family members look at her puzzled.

"Every child should speak at least, one local language. We cannot afford to let our languages and dialects go extinct."

"Can a language go extinct?" Kelechi's mother asks curiously.

"Certainly!" Mrs Ofochi replies. "The other day, I read an article where UNESCO reported on how languages are dying. I got really interested and worried at the same time, so I decided to do some research. I found out that Livonian language no longer exists. Cromarty, a dialect of the Scots is also extinct. Even our neighbouring country, Cameroun has lost a language, Njerep. A language is like a human being. Feed it by speaking it, and it lives. Starve it by not speaking it and it dies."

Uncle Uzo and his wife shake their heads. Enyinna's mother goes on, "When children speak…"

As she talks, Enyinna pulls away Chisom. They have a lot of catching up to do. They have not seen one another in two years.

"I will teach my cousins Igbo while we are here," he resolves.

The caterer soon arrives with her retinue of assistants. The bold inscription on her van—Madam Feed Well Catering Services—amuses Enyinna. She is directed to the far end of the compound and she soon sets to work. Enyinna watches with rapt attention as cups, trays, plates and pots are unloaded from the van. The caterer is a young, beautiful woman, full of smiles. She is dressed in a beautiful red dress which compliments her fair skin. Without any waste of time, she begins to issue instructions to her aides.

"Madam Feed Well, I hope you will really feed us well tomorrow," Uncle Uzo teases her.
"Trust me, you will eat and eat till you beg to eat no more," she responds, with a sweet smile.

Everyone is busy, getting set for tomorrow. An orange-coloured ankara fabric has been used to make clothes for all the grandchildren. Enyinna's mother hands

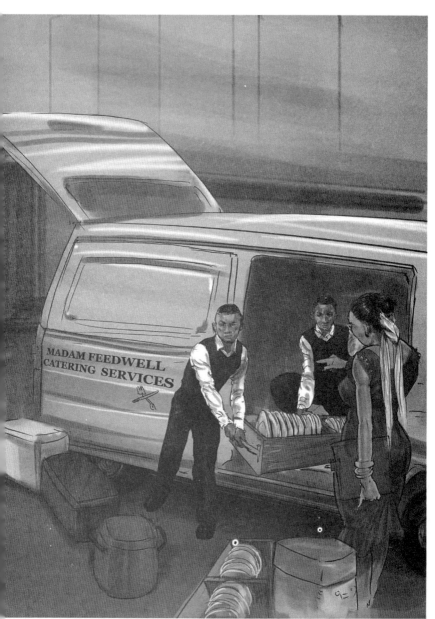

The caterer soon arrives with her retinue of assistants.

each grandchild their own. "Quickly try it on," she instructs them. "If there is any need for an amendment the tailor will do it while he is still here." She keeps Ezinne's cloth aside. It is painful that she could not come. She is writing her first semester exams.

Uncle Uzo supervises the people who are setting up the canopies. Enyinna's dad is making calls, directing his friends on how to get to Owuama. Some will arrive today; others tomorrow. The only hotel in the town has been fully booked by the Ofochi family for their guests. The air is thick with excitement.

Chapter Seven
Sad End to a Great Celebration

Early the next day, Enyinna's mum wakes up all the grandchildren to have their bath. "A lot of people will need to use the bathrooms, so let the children bathe first and get ready," she instructs.

Enyinna and his cousins are full of excitement. They are look beautiful and colourful in their ankara outfit. Mama Nnukwu is clad in a beautiful purple-coloured george wrapper, gold coloured lace-blouse and a gold-coloured pair of sandals. Kelechi's mother assists her with the headscarf.

"Please don't make it too tight. These big scarves give me a headache," she pleads. "You younger women can endure the headaches. I cannot."

Her daughter in-law smiles. "I know Mama. I will make it as comfortable as possible."

Papa Nnukwu emerges from his room looking kingly in his isi-agu attire. It has a shade of purple, to complement Mama Nnukwu's george wrapper.

"Hurry up everyone. We must not be late for church," he

cautions.

The church service did not start on time but the reverend father's sermon was brief. Throughout the duration of the Holy Mass, Enyinna could not help but admire the cleric's glittering white tunic. The cleric praises the old couple for staying together in marriage for fifty years:

"Marriage comes with many challenges but because you placed God first, you were able to triumph over every challenge," he enthuses. Grandpa and Grandma beam with smiles. The congregation claps.

Afterwards, family members, guests and well-wishers trooped to the family house for entertainment. The band is already playing. The music is melodious but Enyinna is unfamiliar with the tunes. It must be music that made waves years ago, from the way the elderly people sway to the beats. Enyinna occupies himself, serving drinks. He is in a very happy mood.

Soon, Grandpa and Grandma are called to the podium to cut the cake. There is no knife. They stand there staring at the cake, smiling. The Master of Ceremony makes a joke out of the funny situation. Guests laugh. Enyinna scurries off to Grandma's kitchen to fetch a knife. All he can find is the sheathed knife.

"If it can slice garden eggs, it can as well cut a cake," he thinks. He takes the knife and rushes out of the kitchen.

By the time he gets to the party arena, the caterer had fetched a cake knife from her van, tied up nicely with ribbons. Enyinna quickly ducks the knife into his pocket. He continues to serve drinks.

A young man beckons to him, "Please get me a drink, just a soft drink."

Afterwards, family members, guests and well-wishers trooped to the family house for entertainment.

Enyinna goes to serve him.

"Oh, that reminds me, my boss sent a gift for your grandparents. Come along with me to the car so I can give it to you." Enyinna is too excited to ask who he is and who his boss is. It does not matter. There are so many guests. He follows him outside the gate and he points down the road, "that's the car over there." They walk towards the car. It is a sports utility vehicle. The man opens one of the back doors.

The present is in the middle of the back seat. It is beautifully wrapped.

"It must be a set of china," Enyinna thinks. "Grandma will love it."

"Go on, get into the car and carry the present out carefully. It is very fragile," the man says, sounding very pleasant. As Enyinna steps into the SUV, the man quickly pushes him in, and sits beside him while another man suddenly emerges from nowhere, rushes into the driver's seat and the car speeds off. Enyinna makes a dash to quickly open the other side of the door to jump out but sadly it is child-locked. He starts to scream but the young man ties up his mouth with a piece of cloth. Enyinna freezes with shock. The windows of the car are tinted and wound up. Nobody can see from the outside and it is already growing dark. Everything has happened in a flash.

He struggles but is overpowered by the man. There is a figure of another man at the back seat of the SUV. He is seated in a slant position, deliberately hiding his face. Enyinna sobs and his body shakes.

"My dear boy, be calm. We won't hurt you. We are just

"If it can slice garden eggs, it can as well cut a cake."

kidnappers. As soon as the merriment of your grandparents' celebration is over, we will call your father to let him know you are in our custody. If he performs and does what we ask for, you will be set free."

Enyinna sobs and moans bitterly.

Chapter Eight
The Search for Enyinna

Enyinna's absence is not noticed until the last guests are gone from the compound. With a heavy yawn, Mrs. Ofochi calls out to her son. When she does not get a response, she calls out to Chisom to check if Enyinna is asleep.

"He really wore himself out today, serving drinks. I am sure he has fallen asleep on any available sofa."

When Chisom came back to report to Mrs. Ofochi that she could not find Enyinna anywhere in the house, she got a bit alarmed.

"Did you check all the rooms?"

"Yes, Ma." The troubled look on Chisom's face gets Mrs. Ofochi panicking. She stands up immediately and dashes off, going from room to room, screaming her son's name. She runs to the back of the compound, her husband following closely behind her. The shouts of "Enyinna" echoes everywhere as everyone joins in the search all over the house, hoping that he had truly fallen asleep somewhere in the compound. There is commotion in the entire household.

"When was the last time you saw him, Chisom?" Uncle Uzo asks trying not to betray his worried expression to his own child. He had run out of the bathroom where he was having a shower, with a towel tied round his waist.

"During the party, Daddy," the girl replies, sobbing. It has been almost four hours since any of them saw Enyinna. Everyone had been swallowed by the day's activities.

At this time, Mrs. Ofochi is sobbing. Her husband tries to calm her.

"Calm down dear. Please, calm down."

"How can I calm down? My son is nowhere to be found. Tell me, how can I calm down?"

Grandma is wailing uncontrollably. She refuses to be comforted. "Enyi m.' Enyi m," she says repeatedly, hitting her hands on her chest. Grandpa rushes off to the town crier's. An announcement has to be made immediately. Uncle Uzo takes his torchlight and walks towards the water tank. Mrs. Ofochi's heart nearly stops beating as she sees her brother-in-law flashing the torch light as he peeps into the big water tank.

"Don't tell me my son has drowned," she screams frantically. Don't tell me Enyi has drowned in the tank of water."

"Enyinna has not drowned, Sisi." Uzo calls his elder brother's wife Sisi, as a mark of respect.

The town crier's metal gong could be heard in the background. He is already making the announcement. 'Ndi be anyi gee nu nti oo.'

"Enyinna, the hero boy, Enyinna the good boy, the city boy who speaks our dialect as if he was born and bred here, Enyinna is missing. All able-bodied men are requested to

"...we must find Enyinna."

gather at the *Nnukwu Nkwo* market square immediately. We are all moving in groups as search parties to look for our son, the boy who has helped many old women to communicate with their children living in the cities. We must find Enyinna."

Young men begin to move to the market square in droves. Many of them are running. Women troop into Grandpa's compound. Some are wailing while some are sobbing. Grandpa, who has come back from the town crier, cautions them sternly, "I don't want to hear any cries here. This is not a house of mourning. Nobody is dead. My grandson is not dead and cannot be dead. God forbid. I cannot bury my own grandson, *tufia*!" he snaps his fingers across his head.

The cries and wailings cease. Except Grandma who still moans softly, a lot of the women echo Grandpa. "God forbid," they all murmur repeatedly.

Meanwhile, the men assembled in the market square are divided into groups. With lanterns, torch lights and sniffing dogs, they all set out, combing every nook and cranny of the town, in search of Enyinna. Darkness has fallen.

Chapter Nine
In the Kidnappers' Den

Throughout the long drive, Enyinna perceives a foul odour in the car. In spite of his sadness and heavy heart, the odour is strong and unpleasant. Everyone in the car is quiet. Enyinna has never been so scared all his life. They have told him that they will not hurt him but this does not stop his fear and anxiety.

After a long, bumpy ride of about two hours, the vehicle eventually screeches to a halt. Enyinna is led out and his mouth untied. He is ordered not to look up as they march him towards a building. The sounds of birds chirping tell Enyinna the house must be in the middle of a forest. The man that has been driving the car leads the way into the house.

"What will you eat?" he demands. Enyinna keeps mute even though he feels very hungry. He had been too busy serving the drinks that he did not bother to eat. He had planned to eat after the ceremony, in a relaxed atmosphere with his cousins. Madam Feed Well had promised him a generous serving of fried rice and salad. Now, he is a kidnap victim. He is too sad to talk. He is thinking of his parents, his grandparents, uncles, cousins and aunts. He is wondering what will be happening

The sounds of birds chirping tell Enyinna the house must be in the mi̇̃̃ of a forest.

now, they must have noticed his absence. A huge man walks into the room and everyone looks up.

"Small boy, what do you want to eat?" Enyinna remains mute. "What will you eat?" the man asks again, impatient.

"Fried rice and salad," Enyinna whimpers.

They all burst into laughter. Enyinna wonders what is causing the laughter.

"See his mouth like fried rice. You think you are in Ikoyi," the hefty man says, still shaking with laughter.

Enyinna is stunned at the remark. "How did he know we live in Ikoyi?" he wonders but manages not to show his surprise. His father had told him several times not to betray his emotions at critical moments. This kidnap is the most critical time of his life and he must play smart, he resolves within himself.

"My dear boy, we only have fufu with bitter leaf soup, bread with sardine and garri with groundnut, so make your choice."

"Bread and sardine," he barely mutters.

As he eats, he thinks of everyone at home. Everyone will be very sad about how the 50th wedding anniversary ended. He feels so bothered about Grandma, remembering how she had wept over her missing goat. "Now with her grandson missing, she will be wailing and sobbing her heart out," Enyinna reasons. Hot tears roll down his cheeks again. He suddenly loses appetite for the food, in spite of his hunger.

"We have spoken to your father. We will let him speak to you later tonight," the hefty man says to him. He seems to be their leader. They all wear face masks.

"How did they get Daddy's number?" he wonders.

The room they put him in is bare, with just a small mattress on the floor, a pillow, a smelly blanket and two oversized t-shirts. He feels another surge of sadness. He fights back the tears.

The next morning, they offer him bitter-leaf soup and fufu. It is a meal he hates to have for lunch or dinner at home, now to have it as breakfast is unthinkable. He manages to eat a little because he is very hungry.

He is confined to the room, with a strict instruction to tap at the door when he needs something. He does not need anything from them. He simply wants to go home. He only taps at the door when he feels pressed. Then someone opens the door to take him to the toilet. It is a dirty and smelly toilet with cockroaches perching all over the walls. The sight of them gives him a creepy feeling.

This afternoon, they serve him beans. It is not well-cooked and Enyinna vomits afterwards. They did not come quickly when he tapped on the door. Before he got to the toilet he had stained his clothes.

He has been on the same clothes ever since his kidnap. Now the clothes are dirty and smelly. He feels even sadder and bursts into tears again. There is nothing to do, nobody to speak to. He just stares at the ceiling, in between tears.

By the morning of the third day, Enyinna feels very sick. He is bored and weary. He has no idea of time except that the sun rises and darkness falls. The days and nights are unusually long for Enyinna. There is nothing to do, nobody to speak to. He just stares at the ceiling, in between tears.

He listens to every sound and movement around him. The kidnappers seem to be very busy at all times. They move in and out of the compound at intervals. Enyinna could tell from opening and shutting of the gate. He hears different voices ᴉing from different parts of the house.

ost times, the conversations are in very low tones but often, ᴄe are sudden bursts of angry voices. There seems to be so ny of them but Enyinna is able to pick up some regular ᴄes. He also picks out a few names; very strange names. He been able to match some of the names with their voices. ᴇre is one called Thunder. He speaks authoritatively. He ᴍs to be their leader. Another one is Mercury. There is also ᴇ called Monster.

ᴉey seem to be having an important meeting today. Thunder ᴉiving them some instructions. "Monster," he thundered, ᴉu will wait at the junction and give us instructions on ᴇn to strike."

ᴇs, Sir."

ᴉnd you, Mercury, make sure you don't mess up things."

ᴇs, Sir."

ᴉunder's voice, even from another room, frightens Enyinna.

ᴇ is complying with all their instructions. They did not ᴉdfold him but he ensures that he does not look at their ᴇs directly. He has no choice. His father always told him ᴉ when an opponent has weapons, the victim must think of life first. He has to do all within his power to stay alive and ᴉ his family soon. He does not know the amount of money ᴉ have demanded from his father as ransom but it must be ᴉ huge. "If the money is not too big, Daddy would have ᴉ them."

ᴉey allow him to speak to his father every day, for just one ᴉute. He assures him that they are almost close to raising ᴉthe money for his ransom. "You will be back home in a

few days, Enyi *m*," his father told him yesterday. He alw
calls him 'Enyi *m*,' and Enyinna is truly his father's friend.
misses his mother desperately and wants to speak to her
the kidnappers won't let him.

He thinks of his sister. Initially, Enyinna had felt v
sad that Ezinne could not come to Owuama. Now, with
kidnap, he is very glad she did not come. Ezinne loves
brother very dearly and would have been so shattered by
event of his kidnap.

To occupy his mind, he decides to replay the tongue-twist
games he always plays with his sister.

"A plantain planter planted plantain in a plantain
plantation."

"The two-toed tiger tried to tiptoe too."

"Fourteen frail friends found firecrackers frightening."

He soon gets tired of the tongue twisters. He tries to sl
but he cannot. He simply stares at the ceiling.

Tonight, they serve him jollof rice and fish for dinner. I
the only decent meal they have offered him since his kidr
He devours the food like a hungry lion. Shortly after, he f
asleep.

Chapter Ten
A Narrow Escape

He is aroused from his sleep by the noise of a heated argument coming from the other room. It is Thunder's voice. He seems to be speaking on the phone with somebody. He sounds very angry.

"I cannot pay you fifty per cent, Jonah," he thunders.

Enyinna freezes with shock. "Could it be our own Jonah or another one?"

Thunder's next words shock him even more.

"Listen Jonah or whatever you call yourself, you are not the first family driver we have used for our operations and you won't be the last. No driver has ever demanded fifty per cent of the ransom."

Enyinna feels hot sweat trickle down his cheeks, in spite of the breeze blowing through the open window. He feels like getting up to tell Thunder that it is a mistake, that it can't be Jonah, his own Jonah, the only family driver he grew up knowing. He calls him 'Uncle Jonah', so does his sister. Enyinna fights hard to stop himself from screaming. The shock is almost too much for him to bear. Thunder is still speakin His voice has dropped a pitch low. Enyinna struggles hard hear.

"Look, you don't know how much it costs me to mainta this house, feeding our captives till their families pay. Yo either take thirty per cent or you forget it," Thunder say hissing.

Then Enyinna hears another voice. He listens harder but th voice sounds very faint and funny. The speaker is apparent trying to pacify Thunder but he still seems very angry.

"Where did you find such a greedy fellow? Better advis him or I'll waste him." Thunder's threat must have frightene the second speaker as he raises his voice this time, soundir alarmed.

"I will talk to him."

Enyinna instantly recognises the squeaky voice. It belong to the limping man with the dark glasses and face ca Enyinna begins to put the pieces together. Jonah's reason fc stopping at Ore to greet the man was simply for the man t identify Enyinna. He also remembers instantly, the unsee person at the back seat of the vehicle on the day of his kidna He recollects the body odour. The picture becomes clearer t Enyinna. It is the same man with the squeaky voice. He mu have stood afar to point Enyinna out to the young man wh asked him for a drink, then quickly came to hide at the bac seat of the vehicle.

He feels so betrayed by the shocking discovery that Jonah part of his kidnap. Jonah that is trusted by his parents. Jona that he loves so much. He feels numb, unable to move. A he lay motionless, staring at the ceiling, his shock graduall gives way to fright and horror.

"They must not kill Jonah," he prays silently. "God, please make him to accept any amount of money that Thunder gives him. I don't want him to be killed."

He hears a door open and shut and he quickly covers himself up with the blanket, pretending to be fast asleep. He hears footsteps coming towards his room, the door squeaks open and a torchlight flashes at him. Then, Thunder mumbles some words that he does not hear, walks off and shuts the door.

Hours later, a car drives in. He hears footsteps, then Thunder's voice commands, "bring her this way." It is obvious that another kidnap victim has been brought into the compound. Enyinna is right because the victim is crying. It is the voice of a woman. She is lamenting that her drugs are not with her. For the whole day, she cries and laments incessantly, pleading with her captors to release her because she is diabetic. Enyinna feels concern for her. She sounds like an elderly woman.

Three days after the woman's kidnap, Enyinna hears the sound of a car driving into the compound. The sound is unusual; like a vehicle with a faulty engine. He hears footsteps of people trooping in. Enyinna instinctively perceives that something bad is about to happen. He had never heard that many feet walking at the same time since he got there. The conversation of the new entrants confirms that.

"Who is in that room?" a deep voice asks, in Igbo.

"The small boy from Lagos," another voice replies.

"The one whose father works for an oil company?"

"Yes."

"So with all the oil money the man has not paid up."

"Maybe he used all his money to throw party in the village."

Enyinna listens keenly, "Thunder's instruction is that we kill the won,
once the money is collected from her family..."

ey laugh.

nyinna's eyes well up in tears at their sarcastic comments but his father. They have moved closer to the window of room but are speaking in very low tones now. Enyinna ains his ears so he can hear them.

But I think the ransom is ready. Thunder will instruct them where to drop it."

"So the little brat will go home any moment from w?"

Of course the little brat will go home but I am not interested that. I am only interested in my share of the money."

Enyinna know they are talking about him. He feels rt that they are calling him a little brat but he is happy that will soon go home. He smiles, for the first time in almost e week.

Ok, so back to the job for tomorrow morning," the deep voice ntinues. Enyinna listens keenly. "Thunder's instruction is t we kill the woman once the money is collected from her nily. It is the safest thing to do."

nyinna opens his mouth in shock. He knew instantly that ey are talking about the elderly woman.

So where do we execute it? Definitely not in this place."

Definitely not," replies the deep voice. "The family is ying her ransom tonight. Once that is done, we will trick r that she is going home to meet her family early tomorrow orning. Then we drive her towards okataka forest, behind e great omigwe cave. That is where the deal will be done."

Enyinna instantly memorises these: 'okataka forest, behind e great omigwe cave.'

"How early?"

"As early as 4 a.m."

Enyinna realises that they are talking about the elde
woman.

"But did she really recognise Mercury on that day we to
her?" another voice asks.

"Mercury swears that she recognised him, even thou
she tried to pretend. Nobody expected that the woman v
recognize him because they had only met once, when Mercu
was working as a security aide to the woman's daughter; w
of the deputy governor.

"So it is safer to get rid of her so that we don't get ii
trouble."

"Exactly."

"What about that driver, Jonah?" one of them asks.

"He is not asking for fifty per cent share anymore. In fact,
says he does not want any money. He claims he has repente
It is the squeaky voice.

"He is chicken-hearted. He should not have gotten involv
at all."

"Now, he wants to put us in trouble with his repentance."

"Anyway, we will waste him too," the deep-voiced m
replies calmly, as if it is indeed a chicken's life that he war
to take.

Enyinna shudders. "They want to kill the woman becau
she recognised one of the kidnappers. They want to kill Un
Jonah because he is backing out. I don't want either the wom
or Uncle Jonah to be killed," he cries inwardly.

Termbling, Enyinna imagines if the elderly woman were to be his Grandma, surely he would do something to save her. "I must save her! But how?" Enyinna wonders, his mind racing with ideas. Just a moment ago, he was very happy to learn that his father is ready to pay the ransom and he will be going home soon. The happiness had died within him immediately he learnt about the plan to kill the woman. He could not get the thoughts out of his mind. The woman's cries and lament in the past few days have moved Enyinna to so much compassion. "I cannot just let them kill her. I must escape tonight and inform the police," he resolves. He looks round the room. Everywhere is bare, except for the mattress, pillow, blanket and two big t-shirts which he never wore.

The planners' voices interrupt his thoughts. One of them is ordered to fetch drinks from the car.

"You know how we do it." They throw banters among themselves, resolving to drink and smoke heavily in order to get themselves ready for the job. The entire conversation has been in Igbo. Enyinna heard and understood everything they said. Soon, Enyinna hears the sound of bottles opening. The drinking spree begins.

About an hour later, Enyinna hears them snoring.

"Could all of them have fallen asleep?"

He earnestly hopes so. It is growing dark. Everywhere is quiet. Even the elderly woman seems to have grown tired of crying and pleading for her drugs.

Enyinna pretends he wants to use the toilet and taps on the door. There is no response. He taps again. Still no one comes to take him. "It is now or never," he resolves, as he embarks on the riskiest venture of his young life, amidst fear and trepidation. The thought of saving the life of the elderly woman is his major concern. "They will embark on the mission to kill her by 4 a.m. tomorrow. If only I can get away fast and inform the police."

He arranges the blanket into the shape of someone sleeping. He rolls the over-sized t-shirts that they gave him as his sleeping cloth into the shape of a human head and places it on top of the pillow. He then gently pushes the door of his room open and gingerly steps into the corridor. The door is bolted and locked with a heavy padlock. He examines the lock. It is rusty. He thinks fast. "If I can unscrew the nuts, I will be able to unbolt the door without tampering with the padlock," he reasons. He looks around for a tool to use. There is none. His heart sinks. The sleeping men can wake up any moment. They may kill him instantly if they catch him trying to escape. Enyinna's heart pounds heavily as he thinks desperately of what to do about the locked door.

Suddenly he remembers something! "The knife," he whispers! "Grandma's knife with the safety sheath." It had been inside his pocket ever since he kept it there during his grandparents' anniversary, during the cutting of the cake. The kidnappers did not discover it. They would have taken it from him. Enyinna hurriedly sets to work. He places the sharp end of the knife carefully in the small hole at the centre of the nut. He begins to unscrew hurriedly. It is going to be a hard task, he knows. There are four nuts in all; old and rusty. He hopes with all his soul that he will be able to finish before they wake up from their drunken sleep. Hot sweat pours down his body.

Finally, he unscrews the last nut and pulls off the bolt gently. He lifts the wooden door slightly before pushing it open, so it does not make noise. He steps out. Darkness has fallen but luckily, the moon is shining. He tiptoes to the end of the compound and crouches down, wondering if he should try to

...it may wake them up and their first instict will be to shoot me dead."

scale the fence or search out the gate key from the pockets of the sleeping men. "That will be too risky. It may wake them up and their first instinct will be to shoot me dead."

He suddenly remembers Orinkemadu's confession of Grandma's stolen goat. He said he was able to scale into Grandpa's compound by climbing the nearby mango tree. He had jumped into the compound, straight from the tree, then unbolted the back gate, through which he took the goat away.

Enyinna looks around the compound but there is no tree nearby. He notices a big drum at the other side of the compound. He tiptoes to the drum and peeps inside. It empty. He carries the drum gently and sets it close to the wall. He looks around hurriedly and sees two big blocks nearby. Panting heavily, he lifts them on top of the drum, to give him more height. He climbs gingerly, remembering his boy scout and taekwondo drills. He gets to the top of the wall and looks over. Luckily, it is mere soil on the other side. Enyinna jumps landing on his knees. He lies down on the sand for a while to regain some strength. He wipes off blood that is beginning trickle from his knees.

Moments later, he gets up and begins to run briskly down the bush path. He does not know where he is running but he just keeps running. Tired from running, he begins walk briskly in the growing darkness, stopping at intervals to catch his breath. He is thirsty, hungry and tired. He also scared; very scared. He feels so lonely. The moon is his only companion. He had sat so many times under the moon to listen to tales from his Grandpa. Tonight, the moon is his guide, throwing some light to him in the dark and lonely bush path. The silence of the night is interrupted by twittering of the birds.

Enyinna sees a fallen tree truck. He sits down on it to rest for while. His head is spinning and his whole body aches. He begins to weep, wondering if he will make it out of the bush alive. "What if I get attacked by a dangerous wild animal?"

"What if I get bitten by a snake?" The thoughts send shivers down his spine. He has heard about dangerous snakes that have their victims dead within minutes. Grandpa has told him about a particular kind of snake, called *echi ete ka*, which means 'tomorrow is too far'. Anyone bitten by *echi ete ka* cannot live to see the next day because the venom from the snake is very deadly. He jumps to his feet and begins to run again, in spite of his aching body. He must get to the police tonight because the elderly woman must not die. Tomorrow will be too late, yes, indeed! *echi ete ka.*

At last, he begins to hear noises of vehicular movements from afar. He walks on, in the direction of the noise. There are bruises on his legs and he is growing very faint. He quietly prays his energy will carry him through to a safe place.

Finally, he gets to a major road. He searches for a sign post, to know the town he is in. "Emenike Provision Store, Umuikpa Town," reads a sign in a block of shops across the road. The owner of the shop is locking up for the night. Enyinna dashes across the road to meet him. "Please take me to the police station," he pleads. "They must not kill her." The man looks puzzled. Enyinna's dirty appearance gets the man suspicious. He quickly padlocks the door of his shop. He knows what street urchins can do. He cannot allow any dirty-looking rascal to make away with his goods or money.

"They must not kill who?" he asks in disdain, wondering if the boy standing before him has a mental problem. Enyinna hurriedly narrates his ordeal.

Settling Enyinna gently at the back of his motor-cycle, Emenike, the shop owner, drives speedily to Umuikpa police station. Enyinna clasps his hands tightly around Emenike's waist. He is not used to riding in a motor-cycle. Upon arriving at the station, Emenike leads the thoroughly weak Enyinna by the hand to the officers on duty. The clock hanging on the wall shows it is almost midnight. Enyinna's heart races as he spurts out: "Okataka forest, behind the great omigwe cave. Please you must save her." Emenike takes over the narration as Enyinna collapses on the chair.

The police officers swing into action immediately.

Chapter Eleven
A Hero's Welcome

Enyinna was brought back home by some of the police officers from Umuikpa station. Owuama and Umuikpa are in different local government areas of the state. The officers were very pleased with Enyinna, for his brave acts.

The joy of Enyinna's return is visible on everyone. People are trooping into the compound in great numbers. It is like another celebration. Mrs. Ofochi hugs her son endlessly, tears of joy streaming down her face. His father lifts him to his shoulders and dances round the compound as Enyinna shrieks with delight. He sets him down, holds him in a tight embrace and mutters affectionately "Welcome home. I have truly missed you, my son and my friend." On rare moments like this, Mr. Ofochi reiterates the meaning of his son's name, Enyinna-father's friend.

Grandma and her friends dance tirelessly. Nne Ugomma throws her walking stick aside to join in the dance. The pain on her leg seem to have been suspended, to allow the old woman to celebrate Enyinna's safe return.

Udoka, the town crier's son runs into the compound on

hearing about Enyinna's return. He has wept every day since Enyinna's kidnap, hoping and praying for his eventual return. He presents Enyinna with a gift. It is a flute, which he carved by himself. Enyinna is very pleased to receive the gift. He is even more pleased to see Udoka on one of the outfit he gave him. He promises to invite him over to Lagos soon. Udoka is thrilled at the idea of visiting Lagos.

"Don't worry. I will talk to my parents about it and I am sure they will let you come. My dad will arrange for your transportation."

Udoka nods happily.

The traditional ruler of Owuama arrives with his council members to welcome Enyinna. Igwe, as the traditional ruler is known, addresses the crowd.

"Enyinna has done very well. I am proud of him. He is a true son of Owuama and that is why I have come personally to give him a hero's welcome. He is indeed a hero."

The crowd clap boisterously. Igwe continues. "What is happening these days is very strange. Our children cannot speak our language anymore. You see a rare case here. Enyinna's knowledge of his mother tongue made him know the kidnappers' plans. He risked his life to save the life of an elderly woman. I hope that other parents would learn from this. Wherever you live, you must teach your children their mother tongue. It is very important. Our language must not die."

"Igweeeee!"

The crowd chorused at the end of the traditional ruler's speech. Enyinna is presented with the traditional red cap, a symbol of recognition by the Igwe and members of his council, for his heroic deeds. His parents beam with smiles. They are proud their son. Enyinna beams with smiles.

ust then, a convoy of cars drive into the compound. Everyone ɔks on in curiosity as people begin to emerge from the cars.

Where is the brave boy who saved my life?" Enyinna stantly recognises the voice of the elderly woman. He steps ·ward and the woman scoops him into her arms.

I have come with my family members to pay a 'thank you' ʒit. Thank you, my son. Thank you very much." Her children ɛe turns to thank Enyinna and his parents. "I was told to y back in the hospital but I refused. I said I must come to ɛ you and your parents before you return to Lagos."

he most gorgeously dressed woman amongst them roduces herself.

'I am Mrs. Ada Nwaoku, wife of the Deputy Governor. My ɔther's kidnap was very distressing to our entire family ɔecially because of her health challenge. We are very happy ₄t she was saved at the point of being killed. Enyinna, we · very happy with your brave act. You are indeed a hero. ɛe police officers at Umuikpa told us everything. The ɔrmation you gave them about otakata forest led them to ₄est the evil men."

ɲe beckons to her aides and they begin to bring out items m the cars. There are crates of drink, baskets of assorted it, bags of rice, tubers of yam and bunches of plantain.

₄We cannot pay you back Enyinna, but we have brought ·se items for your family as a token of our appreciation."

ɲe opens her bag and brings out a beautifully-wrapped ₄. "This, is for you my dear," she says handing the gift to ·yinna. "It is a wristwatch. I hope you like it."

Thank you very much, ma," Enyinna replies smiling. He is

Enyinna is presented with a feather cap, a symbol of recognition by the Igwe amd members of his council, for his heroic deeds.

full of joy for all the honour given to him, all in one day.

Before Mrs. Nwaoku departed with her entourage, they discussed the importance of running security checks on domestic staff. "It is a former security aide of mine that betrayed us."

"Our case is similar," Mr. Ofochi remarks sadly. "Our driver whom we trusted so much did this to us."

Mrs. Ofochi sighs deeply, too overwhelmed to comment on Jonah's greed and act of betrayal.

Chapter Twelve
The Language Club

The Ofochis makes their journey back to Lagos two days after Enyinna's return. Mr. and Mrs. Ofochi are happy that their son came out of captivity safe and sound. The event of the kidnap has shaken them like nothing ever did, ever since their marriage.

They are in Onitsha, just before the River Niger bridge when Enyinna sees the newspaper headline: 'Kidnap Syndicate Rounded Up.'

"Daddy call the vendor fast! Buy the papers." Mr. Ofochi slows down and beckons to the vendor. He pays for two copies of the papers. His wife grabs a copy while his son takes hold of the other. Right on the front page are pictures of Jonah and the rest of the gang. The story details their evil activities and how a brave boy's action led to their arrest. They are in police custody and will be charged to court soon. For security reasons, Enyinna's name and other details were left out in the story.

The three are quiet for a while, but each in deep in thought. The object of their thought is Jonah and his wicked act.

"He has chosen his path and will face the full wrath of the law," Mr. Ofochi says finally.

Back to school in Lagos, Enyinna diligently wrote his essay, "How I spent my Holiday." He narrated the entire event of his kidnap and escape. He pointed out that his knowledge of the Igbo language enabled him to know what went on at the kidnappers' den.

He is swept off his feet when his essay is declared as the best. He is called out at the school assembly and presented with a prize. The news of his kidnap and heroic escape quickly spread round the school. The teachers are quite impressed that his knowledge of Igbo made this possible.

Few days after, Enyinna talks to some of his classmates about the idea of setting up a language club. "This is to promote speaking of local languages by students."

"So how do we go about it?" Ibrahim asks, sounding very interested.

Enyinna goes on to explain his plans in detail.

"First of all, we need to get the entire class to buy into the idea. We will begin amongst ourselves. We will set aside one day in the week to learn different Nigerian languages. Each person will teach the rest of the class basic words of their language. For instance, Ronke and Segun, being Yoruba will teach us greetings, songs and the alphabet in Yoruba. Efe and Ejiro, being Urhobo will do the same, and so on. We will then tell this idea to the entire school."

"But the head teacher must be informed," Efe suggests.

"Certainly. We will inform him," Enyinna responds.

"What about those who cannot even speak a word of their language?" Segun asks, sounding worried. He does not speak

Yoruba. His mother is Ibibio and his Yoruba father hardly stays at home because of his business. Segun does not speak Ibibio either. His mother who would have taught him cannot speak it too. She was born and bred in England.

"That is the fun part of it. Those who cannot speak it will be helped and taught by those who can." Enyinna has thought out everything.

"The only thing I know how to say in Urhobo is *migwo*," Ejiro says laughing hilariously.

"I will coach you," Efe assures her.

They agree to see the head teacher immediately to tell him of their plans. Mr. Sobo is very happy with the idea.

"You have my full support for this noble idea. We have to invite students and teachers from other schools to the inauguration. We will also invite relevant authorities and officials from both the ministries of education and culture."

Enyinna is glad at the way things are moving. Every day, at break time, he meets briefly with his friends to discuss plans for the inauguration of the club.

"Can we ask the Fine Arts teacher to help us design beautiful banner for the club?" Efe suggests in one of the planning meetings.

"Good suggestion!" Enyinna exclaims, taking notes. "And our slogan will be boldly written on the banner."

"What is the slogan going to be," Ibrahim inquires curiously.

"Our languages must not go extinct!" He has not forgotten his mother's discussion with Kelechi's parents at Owuama. The word 'extinct' has stuck to his memory.

His friends clap. The slogan is adopted at once.

He is called out at the school assembly and is presented with a prize.

On the day of the inauguration, the school hall is filled with parents and other dignitaries. Enyinna and his classmates have worked very hard to see that everything is in order. Their teachers have been very cooperative too.

Officials from the state Ministries of Education and Culture are in attendance. There is also an official from UNESCO. Some members of the press are also in attendance.

The head teacher does a brief introduction:

"This event is very important and necessary because of the current trend in our society. A lot of children who live in cities hardly speak our local languages any more. It is quite disturbing. The Language Club, being inaugurated today will help arrest the trend."

The official from UNESCO speaks next. He enumerates some of the efforts the organization is making towards ensuring that local languages stay alive. He also states that February 21 every year is international mother tongue day. He suggest that the language club should celebrate this annual event.

Enyinna beams with smiles as he is called up to the podium and announced as the pioneer president of the club. He received a lot of praises for his noble idea in initiating the club. As the cameras clicks away, his mind races back to the events of the last few weeks. He thinks about the power of language not only to save a life but also to bring harmony and love to a community.

THE END

Glossary of non-English words and phrases used in the book

Chapter One

Ututu oma: Igbo phrase for 'good morning'

Nwa m: Igbo phrase for 'my child'

Kedu: Igbo word for 'how are you?'

Ugu: Igbo name for the leaves of the fluted pumpkin plant.

O di mma: Igbo phrase for "I am fine"

Akara: bean cake fried in hot oil

Akamu: porridge made from corn, usually eaten with akara

Edikang ikong: a special dish of the Efik people of Nigeria, cooked with a lot of vegetable.

Chapter Two

ili nwayo: Igbo phrase for 'take it easy'

Nnoo: Igbo word for 'welcome'

Obi: A sort of small hall where the head of a family stays to receive visitors in Igboland.

Abacha: a meal made from cassava flakes, eaten mainly by Igbo people.

Ikwa: A special meal made from breadfruit, eaten mainly by Igbo people.

Chapter Three

Akpa nkoro: a popular game among Igbo children

Kuru mmiri, kuru azu: a moonlight game played by some Igbo children

Ifo chakpii: an Igbo phrase to begin a folk tale

Noo: the refrain to 'Ifo Chakpii'

Chapter Four

Une nno: welcome ma

O nwa m: yes, my child

Bute oche:	get a chair
Okwa ose kwanu:	what of the groundnut paste?
O gwugo:	It is finished

Chapter Five

Alu eme:	an abomination has occurred
Ndi be anyi gee nu nti o:	Our people, listen attentively

Chapter Six

Ankara:	a kind of fabric, popularly worn in Nigeria

Chapter Eight

Tufia:	Igbo expression signifying that something is an abomination

Chapter Twelve

Mi gwo:	A greeting of the Urhobo people of Nigeria

Questions and Discussions
Chapter One

1. Are you involved in house chores in your home?
2. What are some of the chores you do at home?
3. What is your favourite food for breakfast, lunch and dinner? Do you know how to prepare them?
4. Are you familiar with greetings in your local language?

Chapter Two

1. If you live in the city, discuss among your friends how often you visit your home town.
2. Are you familiar with some towns and cities in Nigeria? Write down some of the towns you have visited within Nigeria.
3. Enyinna is captivated by the beauty of the Niger bridge and the serenity of the River Niger. Do you

know the story of Mungo Park and the 'discovery' of River Niger?

Can you name other rivers in Nigeria and Africa?

Chapter Three

Do you know of any outdoor games in your locality?

Have your parents or grandparents ever told you a folk tale?

Can you recount some of the stories?

What are some of the moral lessons you learnt in the folk tales you have been told in the past?

Chapter Four

When Nne Ugomma came, Enyinna did something as a show of respect. Can you identify what he did?

How will you describe Enyinna's entire actions in this chapter?

Are your grandparents educated? Do you speak English, Pidgin English or your native language with them?

What action(s) will you take towards learning a Nigerian language? If you already speak one, can you try to learn another? You can also encourage your friends to speak their languages if do not.

Chapter Five

Have you ever lost something precious or had it stolen? How did you feel about it?

What are the functions of a town crier in a community?

Enyinna offers some of his clothes to Udoka. Can you recount an act of kindness you have shown to someone recently?

Do you feel some sympathy for the innocent goat buyer, if so why?

Chapter Six

1. Write about an important event which you have attended in the past.

2. Were you part of the preparation for the event? How did you feel on the eve of the event?

3. Ask your parents and grandparents if they will like to celebrate the silver jubilee and golden jubilee of their marriages. Discuss and plan with them on how the event will be.

4. Uncle Uzo is Igbo, his wife is Ijaw. Are your parents from different tribes? If yes, which of the languages do you speak; your dad's or your mum's?

Chapter Seven

1. Enyinna is unfamiliar with the music being played during the party but some older people swayed to the beat. Find out from your parents and older relatives the kind of music they played and enjoyed in their younger days.

2. Do you think it was right or wrong for Enyinna to have followed the stranger to the car in the given circumstance? Give reasons for your answer.

3. Can you describe the following features of a car: back seat, child-lock, tinted windows?

4. What is the reason for a child-lock device in a car?

Chapter Eight

1. Uncle Uzo did not want to betray his worried expression to his own child. Do you understand what 'betray' means in this sentence? You can consult the dictionary to check this out. You may also ask from your teacher.

2. The shouts of "Enyinna" echoes everywhere. What do you understand by the term 'echo'?

3. Have you ever been part of a search party?

4. What are the necessary items you consider important to be taken along during a search?

Chapter Nine

The kidnappers offer Enyinna the following food choices: fufu with bitter leaf soup, bread with sardine and *garri* with groundnut. Have ever eaten any of these food combinations?

When Enyinna thought of his grandma, he suddenly lost appetite for the food he was eating. What can make you lose appetite for food?

Enyinna indulged in tongue twisters while at the Kidnapers' den. Can you play some tongue-twisting games with your class mates or siblings?

How do you keep yourself occupied when you are bored?

Chapter Ten

Enyinna discovers that Jonah is part of his kidnap. Have you ever felt betrayed by a trusted person? How did you feel?

In what ways do you think children can guard themselves against being kidnapped?

Have you ever been in danger? What actions did you take to escape the danger?

Emenike the shop keeper initially thought that Enyinna was a miscreant. Do you know why he thought so?

Chapter Eleven

What is the traditional ruler of your town known as? Can you make a list of the titles of traditional rulers and kings of the different tribes in Nigeria?

Udoka gives Enyinna a flute as a gift. Have you ever seen a wooden flute before? Can you play a flute?

Write down other forms of traditional dance instruments that you are familiar with? Can you play some of them?

Chapter Twelve

Can you recount a remarkable essay you have written in the past?

2. How did you spend your last holiday?
3. Have you ever been called out in your school's assembly ground for something outstanding? Write about it.
4. Discuss with your classmates, the idea of setting up a language club in your school for the promotion of Nigerian languages.

Acknowledgements

I appreciate God for the ceaseless creative bud in me. I owe Him a ceaseless praise.

For putting the icing on the cake of *A Hero's Welcome*, my appreciation goes to several people. Temitayo Olufinlua, for the meticulous editing and for fine-tuning the story. I also thank Dr. Carol Anyagwa for her scrupulous observation and corrections. Olorunfemi Adedeji for the cover design, page layout and many useful ideas and suggestions. Dr. Bosede Afolayan, for going through the initial draft and giving valuable insights. My dear comrade and award-winning children's book author, Adeleke Adeyemi, aka Mai Nasara, thanks for the wonderful feedback you gave after you read the initial draft. Wale Adebiyi, thank you for being an amazing illustrator and for always delivering in spite of crazy deadlines. Mercy Ibekwe and Damilola Isiaka; wonderful staff that have offered me great support. Thanks to you both.

To all the school owners, head teachers, pupils and parents who make my books their choice, I doff my hat for you all. Thanks for being a part of my motivation to write. Kudos to my husband and my children for chipping in their thoughts whenever I needed a second opinion. My mother, siblings, cousins, nephews and nieces: I love the way you show me love. It is reciprocated, even more. Ugonna, dear nephew; special thanks to you, for that night you stayed up late with me, proof-reading *A Hero's Welcome*.